Attack of the Cheeseburgers

Upon the hill
if you know where to look,
sits a castle
carved completely from carrots.

Inside the castle who do we see?
The carrot king and a strawberry.

A pair of pears, an orange that's sweet.
A leek, some corn, but wait….

...There is one empty seat!

Up stood the beetroot named Toot
who wore two purple boots,
who waved his beetrooty arms
in their beetrooty manner;
"Where oh where is Princess Anna Banana."

The pair of pears peered
up and peered down.

They peered high and peered low
and then started to frown.
Their beloved princess
was nowhere to be found.

Terry the strawberry was very surprised.
How could a yellow princess go missing,
right in front of their eyes?

The king ran down the hall,
to look over the wall.
Had he heard a scream?
Did the princess fall?

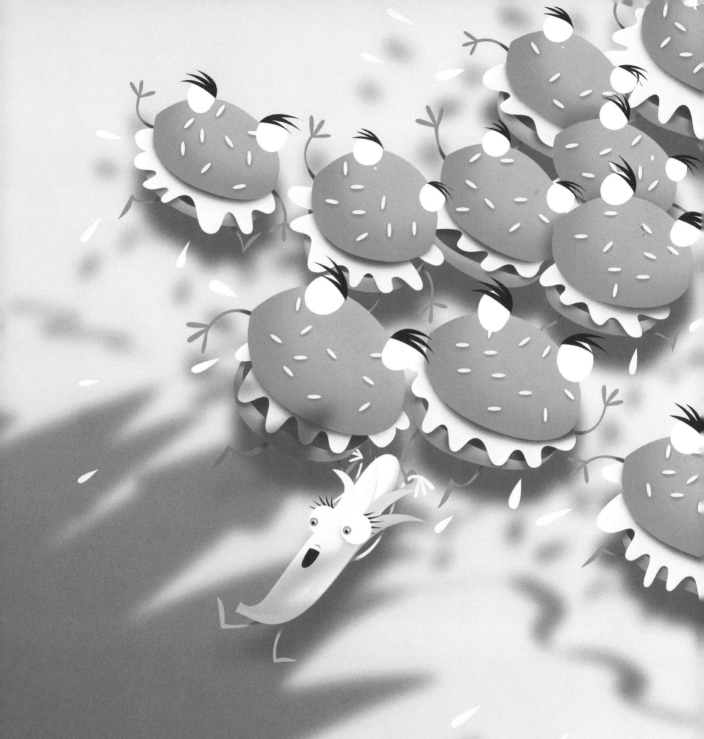

The king looked on in horror, his
princess was being taken away, by a greasy
bunch of cheeseburgers who love to
eat bananas, each and every day.

The king ran down,
the chase had begun.

The fruit and vegetables
had all started to run.

The cheeseburgers left grease,
slimy and smelly.
The grease dripped out
straight from their bellies.

The burgers ran fast
they were thinking of lunch.
But why stop at one banana,
when they could have the whole bunch.

The leader of the cheeseburgers
pushed Princess Anna Banana
to the ground when he saw
the king had caught up to him

"I hope you like cheese"
said the leader.

"I hope you like grease.
I will eat you right up princess.
It will be a real banana feast!"

The king shouted out with all of his might.
It was so loud that even the
cheeseburgers got a fright!

"LET THE PRINCESS GO!"

The cheeseburgers burped and cheese
sploshed on the ground.

They laughed greasy laughs when
they all turned around.

"You think you are loud, you sound like
a parrot. And what we love most of
all is the fine taste of carrot."

"So come here king, we will eat your crown and when we are finished, we will eat your whole town!"

It was at that moment that the king realised
he had made a terrible mistake.

The king looked up, looked high in the air,
he wondered if the sky could hear him,
from way up there.
"Please sky if you can hear me, please
help us, please do. You see all these burgers,
do you know what to do?"

The sky did all it could. it turned
dark and it grumbled.
It fizzed and it cracked and out of the clouds,
the rain started to tumble.

The rain was what the fruit needed to give the fruit and vegetables strength.

It made the cheeseburgers
soggy and weak.

The burgers once scary were now
sloppy and weary. They ran and they slipped
and they all fell to bits. They tried to escape,
but there was nowhere to run.
The cheeseburgers were now no more
than a bun.

The fruit and vegetables gathered, they
threw the princess high in the air.
And as the cheeseburgers melted the
sky started to clear.

The kingdom was free, from the greasy bunch
and the king was glad that he and the
princess had not become lunch.

The End

CPSIA information can be obtained
at www.ICGtesting.com
Printed in the USA
BVHW020623091118
532623BV00030BA/150/P